dick bruna

miffy
in the
tent

World International

Miffy got up one sunny day

and to her mother went

the weather's lovely, Miffy cried

can we put up the tent?

Yes, that is fine, her mother said

a very good idea

I think it should go on the grass

let's put it over here.

It was a very jolly tent

its walls were bright and new

the flap in front could fold right back

enough to let you through.

It had a window at the back

that you could open wide

and shut again if it was cold

with tapes upon the side.

I'll go and make some sandwiches

for you, said Miffy's mum

and you can eat them in the tent

hurrah, said Miff, what fun!

So Miffy, snug inside the tent

sat eating on the ground

but suddenly, what's that? she cried

I'm sure I heard a sound.

She scrambled quickly to the door

and stuck her head outside

now I can see what I could hear

I see it, Miffy cried.

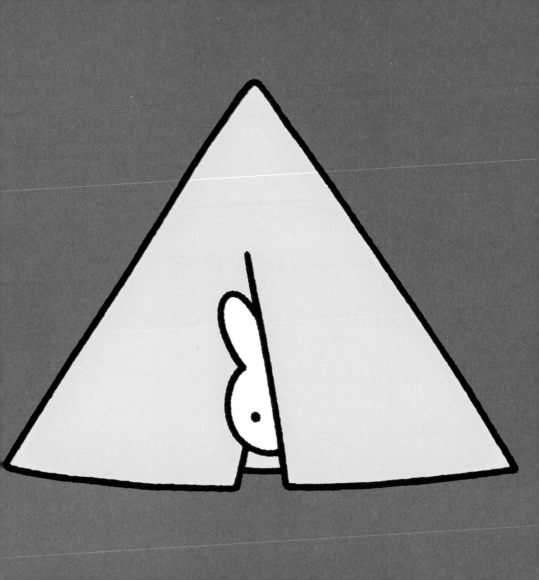

Hurrah, she shouted, oh hurrah

now what did Miffy mean?

her mother, blowing up the pool –

that was what Miff had seen.

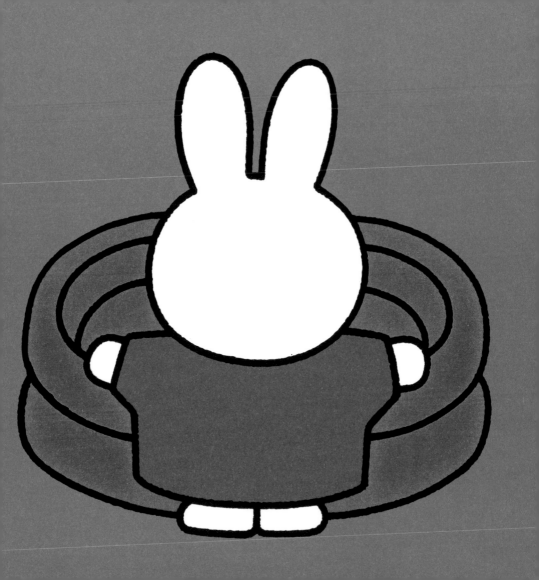

So Miffy took off all her clothes

she had not many on

there now, said Miffy, that is that

I'll paddle in the sun.

The water was so lovely, too

so clear and fresh and cool

and Miffy splashed and laughed

and splashed a long time in the pool.

When she came out she dried herself

at once from top to toe

the towel was so warm and soft

it made her body glow.

Then Miffy went back to the tent

and pulled the window to close

and Miffy was so sleepy now

she fell into a doze.

miffy's library

"nijntje in de tent"
Original text Dick Bruna 1988 © copyright Mercis Publishing BV.
Illustrations Dick Bruna © copyright Mercis BV 1988.
Published in Great Britain in 1997 by World International Ltd.,
Deanway Technology Centre, Wilmslow Road, Handforth, Cheshire SK9 3FB.
Original English translation © copyright Patricia Crampton 1996.
Publication licensed by Mercis Publishing BV, Amsterdam.
Printed by Sebald Sachsendruck Plauen, Germany. All rights reserved.
ISBN 0-7498-2988-5